Thirty-five Years

This book is dedicated to my grandad, Jeff Johnson.
Rest in peace, grandad x.

Contents:

Chapter one: Yasmin

My name is Yasmin and I'm thirty-five years old. I'm a singer and songwriter from Kensington in London. I wrote my first song when I was a young teenage girl. I've always loved singing - even when I was a little girl. It even says about it in one of my school reports from when I was at primary school many moons ago. *"Yasmin enjoys taking part in music lessons. She has taken part in a wide variety of musical experiences - including singing, dancing and composing. She is developing her musical techniques and is becoming more confident in all areas of music. She enjoys exploring the instruments and composing in small groups".* I don't think that anyone really thought that I'd make it as a singer and songwriter, though. I think that most people probably thought that I'd just work in some shop somewhere, and scan items all day long. Not that there's anything wrong with doing that for a living. I know people that do that. These people are my friends - some of my best friends, in fact. Of course, I do have friends that are singers and famous like me. Some may say that we are quite alike. Some may think that I have it all: the money, the fancy designer clothes and the big house in the city. I admit that yes, I do have those three nice things and more, but what I don't have that a lot of people have - including my friends - is children.

This is something that I have always, always wanted, but haven't gotten yet. It actually makes me feeling kinda sad when I see my friends with their partners and little ones. Currently, I don't have any children and I certainly don't have a partner. Admittedly, there have been guys that I once thought would make a good, loving partner that I would happily spend the rest of my life with, but I was far too shy to say anything to them about my feelings for them. Seven years ago, there was a guy called Matt who I really did thought was the one. He was thirty-one at the time, and I was twenty-eight, so there wasn't much of an age difference there, but like I said, I was far too shy to say anything to them about my feelings for them. Me being shy - despite being a famous singer and songwriter - might come as a shock and a surprise for some people - people that don't know me from Adam, but those close to me know just how shy I can be sometimes in certain situations. An example of this is when it comes to paying for stuff at the till in stores. I always try and get other people to do stuff like that for me so that I don't have to. Some might laugh at this, but do I care? No... Okay, maybe yes. I care about a lot of things - sometimes a little too much. Another thing I care about is "likes" on the posts that I put up online. I sometimes worry that I don't have that many likes and don't look "popular enough".

Chapter two: Love Hearts and Lies

Another guy who I thought was the one was a guy who I had been talking to online. He told me that he loved, liked and appreciated me. He also sent me red love heart emojis. He made me feel loved and special, but then I found out that he was seeing someone else the whole entire time, so I felt like his dirty little secret - which I hated and felt hurt about, as you can imagine. To take my mind off of the hurt that he had caused, and to turn this situation into something positive, I wrote a song about it and released it. It's called 'Love Hearts and Lies', and It goes like this: *"At first, I loved you, but now just I hate you. You told me that you appreciated me, liked me and loved me – sending me little red heart emojis. You said that you were single and still living the bachelor life, but that was all just a big, fat lie, lie, lie. Because all you do is just lie, lie, lie – sending me more red heart emojis and telling me more lies, lies, lies. Why did you feel the need to lie, lie, lie to me? I did not deserve that. At first, I loved you, but now just I hate you, because all this time, you've been secretly seeing somebody else – living in your house with somebody else. At first, I didn't want to be with anybody else, but then I found out that you were secretly seeing somebody else. You were just telling me more lies, lies, lies. I hope that you're happy and that you've finally found the one. At first, I thought that you really were the one. You told me that you appreciated me, liked me and loved me – sending me little red heart emojis. You said that you were single and still living the bachelor life, but that was all just a big, fat lie, lie, lie. Because all you do is just lie, lie, lie – telling me more lies, lies, lies. Why did you feel the need to lie, lie, lie to me? I guess this is good bye, bye, bye. No more of your lies, lies, lies, because now I'm cutting all ties, ties, ties – sick of all of your lies, lies, lies. I didn't deserve any of your lies, lies, lies. I deserve better and that's what I'll get. Goodbye and God bless. No more stress, no more sadness. I'm putting an end to all of this madness. Moving on is hard, but I have to move on from you. You were no good for me and I deserve better than you, so goodbye to you, and hello to better".* I just wrote about how I felt at the time after he did what he did to me. I knew that I really needed to move on from him, even though it was hard to - really hard. He might have been hard to move on from, but I knew that I had to. I deserved better - FAR BETTER - than him. I'm worth a MILLION of him. I always will!

Chapter three: Naomi

I'm not an only child, though there have been many times where I wished that I was. I have a sister named Naomi and she's two years younger than me, so there's not much of an age gap between us. I used to sing about her and say: *"Naomi smells like pepperoni".* She hated it, and used to always run off crying to mum and dad. 'Mum, dad, Yasmin just sung a song about me, saying that I smell like pepperoni when I quite clearly don't. I smell like flowers and perfume and all things nice'. She would say. Her annoying, whiny little voice used to go right through me. Then I'd have mum and dad's loud, angry voices shouting at me, and telling me to stop being so mean to my sister. All I used to say in response to this is: "oh, whatever! She's just jealous of my talented singing voice. Ignore her". As you can imagine, this made Naomi even more mad at me. "I'm not the slightest bit jealous of you, Yasmin. You sound like a cat peeing on a tin when you sing. I however, do not sound like a cat peeing on a tin. I don't know why you're saying that when you know fully well that I'm the better singer out of the two of us!" Naomi would say, even though she doesn't even sing that much and doesn't want to be a singer when she grows up like I do. She wants to be a baker instead. She likes baking with mum and dad at the weekends when there's no school. She tells this awful joke and finds it hilarious, when it really isn't. "How do you know that an elephant had been in the fridge?" She would ask and mum and dad would say that they don't know, even though she'd told this joke like a million times before in the past. "Because of the footprints in the butter!" She would say, laughing. Another thing that I found annoying about her was her laugh. I hated it, but anyway, back to the baking. Sometimes mum, dad and Naomi would all make some orange biscuits out of mum's cookbook together. "Right, so we'll need some butter, plain flour, salt, baking powder, an egg, caster sugar, vanilla essence and oranges – which we've all got on the table right here in front of us, as you can see... Okay, let's get baking!" Mum would say, clapping her hands. "Yay!" Naomi would say, as she punched the air. "So, after we've made these, we'll be able to keep these for five days, as long as we put them in an airtight container, okay?" Mum would say. "Okay, no problems, mama. We've got this, haven't we everyone?" Naomi would say. "Yeah". Dad would reply. "Good. Okay, so if you start doing the first bit, Naomi – which is weighing the butter, that's a good girl". Mum would say. "That's a good girl". I would mock. "Don't say that to your sister, Yasmin. Be nice or go away. The choice is yours. Now apologize to your sister at once!" Mum would say – stood there with her arms folded. She was being serious when she did that.

Chapter four: Baker

Now, as you know, my sister Naomi likes to bake. I used to call her Master Baker, and she used to go berserk and say: "I'm not a master baker! Don't call me that and stop being so mean to me all of the time, Yasmin". Then she would do what she did best, and tell on me to mum and dad so that they would yell at me. That was all a long time ago now, though. Me and my sister, Naomi get on just fine. We sometimes go out shopping together here in London. She now owns her own bakery called *'Beautiful Bakes'.* Whenever she sees me, she always brings me some of her *'Beautiful Bakes'.* She brings some for herself too - and for mum and dad when she visits them at their house. They all still like eating orange biscuits. Even my sister Naomi has children of her own - two girls called Bella and Natasha. They sometimes come along too when we go shopping here in London. I always treat them and buy them nice things. If they want it, I buy it for them. Naomi says that I don't have to do this, but I want to do this. That's why I do this. They're my nieces and I love them both dearly. Not only does it put a smile on their little faces, but on mine too. Their faces light up when I buy them the things that they both want. They go home with bags full of goodies. 'You spoil them way too much, Yasmin. They're both lucky to have you in their lives'. My sister, Naomi says this every time I buy my nieces, Bella and Natasha something. 'And I'm lucky to have them in my life, Naomi. I just wish that I had children of my own to spoil way too much like I do with Bella and Natasha'. I say. 'Don't give up, Yasmin. When the time is right, it'll happen. Not a second too early and not a second too late, but trust me, it WILL happen. You've just got to stay positive and know that it will happen at the right time with the right person. The universe will serve you whatever you want if you truly believe that you deserve it. Visualise and believe, Yasmin, that's the secret. You'll get your desire if you do this, trust me on that one. I know what I'm talking about here'. Says Naomi - which is true, she does know what she's talking about. I decide to give what she said a go, and do all of the visualising and believing stuff. Afterall, it worked for her. I mean, look at her, she's got the two beautiful, healthy and happy children, she's got a man in her life who loves her unconditionally. If she can have it, then I can too! I deserve to have the things that she does right now, and I'm going to do everything I can possibly do to make it happen. Ideally, I would have a man in my life who loves me unconditionally, but as long as I have a child that is healthy and happy, then I don't care about having a relationship with a guy. Afterall, I don't have to be in a relationship with one to have a child of my own. All this time I have been waiting.

Chapter five: Waiting and Wasting

All this time I have been waiting to find the right guy and have a family with him when I really didn't have to. Waiting and wasting, waiting and wasting, waiting and wasting. Well, not anymore! Yes, I'll do exactly what my sister, Naomi says, but if not, then I shall simply have to things another way, because I'm not getting any younger, you know. I'm thirty-five years old now. My biological clock is well and truly ticking. That evening, when my sister, Naomi and my nieces, Bella and Naomi had both gone back home and I knew that they had made it back safely, I started to visualise exactly what I wanted to happen in life – focusing a lot on having children. I visualised holding them in my arms for the first time. I also visualised being with a man who truly loves me and accepts me for who I am and doesn't try to change me in any way. I want a guy who isn't just with me because of what I do for a living or for the money, designer clothes and the nice, big house in the city. I'm really not asking for much here. Naomi says that it's important to visualise every single detail of my desire: what I can smell, taste, touch and see. I do all of these things as best as possibly can. I really want these things to happen and I'm willing to do whatever it takes to make them all happen. Another thing Naomi says is to eliminate all and any doubts that I might have – to truly believe that I deserve to have my desire become my reality. I sit in one of the many rooms inside my very big house and visualise my desires. I feel the joy of having them and what I can smell, taste, touch and see. Then my phone rings and I come back to my current reality. I say current, because I know that it won't last forever. Nothing – absolutely NOTHING – lasts forever. I answer my phone, then get straight back to it with the visualising. I decide to make this part of my routine now. Every evening whenever I can, I commit to doing this. I go in the same room at the same time every evening and do what I need to do to make my dreams and desires a reality. I shall never give up no matter what. Of course, there will be some evenings where I shall have to do it later, because of work. I perform on stage in front of thousands of people. I write my own songs so that they're personal to me and not what somebody else has written. Not that there's anything wrong with that. I don't judge anyone. I also don't judge a situation that I have never been in. In my opinion, people should never judge others. Them being judgemental just simply isn't needed, really, is it? Well, that's what I think, anyway... Even when I do eventually have my healthy and happy child, I'll still do the job that I love – which is singing and song writing.

Chapter six: My Friend

Now, as you know, my biological clock is well and truly ticking. Like I said in the previous chapter, chapter five, I'm not getting any younger. I have decided to have a child, but not with a guy that I'm married to, but with my best friend, Henry. Just like me, he's single and isn't with anyone romantically right now. He's not a stranger - which was one really rather desperate option that I once thought about. I did think about going out on a Saturday night and trying to get someone that way, but decided not to in the end after a conversation I had with my best friend, Henry. Thankfully, he's willing to help give me what I want - which is a child. He doesn't have children either. I've told him that he can be involved in the child's life if he wants to. Afterall, it'll be his child too. Bless him, he's not exactly the sharpest tool or the brightest bulb in the box, and he said: "oh, yeah, I hadn't thought of that one" ... In the end, he decided that he would like to be in the child's life and that's completely, one hundred per cent fine by me. After doing what had to be done, it was just a little, tiny bit awkward, so he got dressed and went home or somewhere. I don't actually know where it was that he went to exactly. Desperate times calls for desperate measures, though. I simply did what I felt had to be done. It's not like I can impregnate myself, can I? Things would've been SO much easier if I could've. If I could, I would, trust me. Hey, you know, mentioning impregnating oneself, I think I read once that tortoises can impregnate themselves... Random, I know, but anyway, enough of the tortoises talk. Let's get back to me now. I mean, this book is all about me, right? This book is the first and only book that I intend to ever write - ever. I'm a singer, not an author - though I shall be one when I publish this, won't I? An author and a singer, eh? I think that that sounds pretty impressive, don't you? Anyway, so fast forwarding a little now. So, I'm late on my period it hasn't come as of yet, and so I decide to do a pregnancy test to try and put my mind at rest (hey, that rhymed. I'm a poet and I don't know it!) I am indeed pregnant, halleluiah! I'm just grateful and glad that I don't have to do what I did with my friend, Henry again. Mentioning my friend, Henry, he was there when I did the pregnancy test that morning. He was more than a little shocked when he saw the positive pregnancy test. "Wow, I'm going to be a dad" ... He said, with his hands on his mouth and eyes as wide as saucers. Then he sat down and said: "and you're going to be a mum" ... "Yes, finally. I can't quite believe it myself. Look, listen, Henry. You mustn't say a word about this to anyone, okay? Not a single soul must know about this until the three-month part". I said. "The three-month part of what?" Henry asked me.

Chapter seven: Three Months

"The three-month part of my pregnancy, what did you think that I was talking about, Henry?" I said. "I don't know, sorry. I'm just a little shocked, that's all. It's not every day that you're told that you're going to be a dad, is it?" Said Henry. I had to be extra secretive about this pregnancy because of me being in the public eye. I want to keep this a secret for as long as possible, because once this little baby secret of mine comes out, it'll be everywhere and everyone will want to know everything about it. Until then, though, I shall still sing and perform in front of thousands of people like I would do normally if I wasn't pregnant like I am now. Afterall, the more "normal" I keep things, the less the chances that they'll guess and find out in the press. This is probably going to be in all of the magazines and newspapers once the press finds out about this. I don't even tell my parents or my sister, Naomi until the three-month part. Thankfully, the morning sickness isn't that much of a big deal, because I've had hardly any of it as of yet. This makes me think that I'm having a baby girl, because I remember my mum saying that she had hardly had any morning sickness when she was pregnant with me, but she had it a lot with my sister, Naomi - in fact, she had it all the way through until she prematurely gave birth to Naomi at eight months pregnant. I'm hoping that my pregnancy stays exactly how it currently is right now, and like when my mum was pregnant with me - with hardly any morning sickness at all. That would be nice. When the three-month part does finally arrive after what honestly felt like a lifetime, the first people I tell is my parents and my sister, Naomi. There were some rumours circulating in the press about me being pregnant before the three-month part, but I simply denied all rumours that were circulating about me and the baby. Of course, the question on everyone's lips was who the father was. I just said that it was a donor and left it at that. I did however, tell my sister, Naomi the truth. I only told her the truth, though and not anyone else - not even my own parents because I didn't want them to hate me or judge me. My sister, Naomi didn't judge me. 'Well, it's good that the child's father is someone you know and not some random stranger that you met on a Saturday night out somewhere'. Says Naomi. 'So, how did he react to the news? Does he want to be in the child's life or not? Because if not, you do realise that you're going to be a single mum with a child, don't you?' She says. 'I do realise that, but I don't have to worry about that, Naomi, because Henry wants to be involved in the child's life. He was more than a little shocked when he saw the positive pregnancy test. He was like: wow, I'm going to be a dad, and you're going to be a mum'. I say.

Chapter eight: Henry

'Then I said to him: yes, finally. I can't quite believe it myself. Look, listen, Henry. You mustn't say a word about this to anyone, okay? Not a single soul must know about this until the three-month part, and he was like: the three-month part of what?' I add, laughing. 'Oh, bless him, he's not exactly the sharpest tool or the brightest bulb in the box, is he?' Says my sister, Naomi, laughing too now. 'Well, let's just hope that the baby has your brains and not his'. She adds – drinking some of her coffee from the cup. That night, I have my nieces, Bella and Natasha over to stay for the night. 'Now, be good for your auntie Yasmin, okay? I mean it, both of you. When I come and collect the two of you tomorrow, I don't want to be told that you've been naughty. Remember that this is your auntie Yasmin's house and you must both be on your best behaviours. Do you understand?' Naomi says to the girls. 'We understand'. Says Bella and Natasha. 'Good, now I'll see you tomorrow, okay? I love you both to the moon and back, remember that'. Says Naomi, kissing the two girls goodbye and leaving. That night, me and my two nieces, Bella and Natasha have our own little karaoke night, and sing some of my songs and those that are sung by other singers. After a while, though Bella and Natasha stopped singing and just wanted me to sing instead, so I did. I sung one of my songs called *'Don't Give Up',* and it goes like this: *"Don't ever give up, even when you feel like just giving it all up, don't ever give up. Give it one last try. It's okay to be shy, it's okay to cry, but just try - try again and again, and remember that it'll all be worth it in the end. Pretty soon you'll see and you'll be so very glad that you didn't give up. It's okay to get mad, it's okay to need your dad. Just don't ever give up, no matter how hard things get. Pretty soon, you'll be flying in a private jet and be saying about all of the famous people you have met. No longer will you be standing in the cold and wet - wishing that you had a better life. Soon you'll have a loving wife and be living your best life. You deserve the best and that's what you'll get, but only if you don't ever give up and just give it one last try. Apply yourself, push yourself, believe in yourself, be your best self, and don't ever give up - not now, not ever. Now get out there and try your best, because that's all you can do. Remember that you can do this and will do this if you try hard enough and don't ever give up. I believe in you and so should you, so I'm asking you please, don't ever give up. Apply yourself, push yourself, believe in yourself, be your best self, and don't ever give up - not now, not ever. Keep on going, no matter the weather, because it'll all be worth it in the end, I promise"* ... After a night of singing and dancing, Bella and Natasha go to bed.

Chapter nine: Bella and Natasha

During the night, my niece Natasha has a nightmare, so stays in my bed with me - along with her sister, Bella, who decides to join her in the bigger bed. 'Auntie Yasmin, I had a nightmare. Can I stay in the big bed with you, please?' Asks Natasha. 'And me! Can I stay in the big bed too? I promise that I'll be quiet and not take up too much space in the bed'. Adds Bella. 'Alright, you can both get in the big bed. Come and climb on in'. I say, and they do just that. To be fair, they both fall asleep within minutes, so it's okay. Me and Bella wake up the next morning to the sound of Natasha snoring. 'Natasha snores really loud'. Says Bella. After this, me and my nieces all get up, have a wash, brush our teeth, have breakfast and watch *'Peppa Pig'* together until Naomi arrives to pick them up and take them back home. 'So, were you both on your best behaviours like I told you to be yesterday? Were you both good little girls for your auntie Yasmin?' Naomi asks Bella and Natasha when she arrives. 'Yes, mummy, we were'. Says Bella and Natasha. 'Were they both good?' My sister, Naomi asks, looking up at me. 'Yes, they both were. We had karaoke night and did some dancing. Then the girls stopped singing, and just wanted me to sing instead, so I did'. I say. 'Oh, nice. That sounds fun! Well, I'm glad that Bella and Natasha both behaved themselves. We best be off now. Say goodbye to your auntie Yasmin, girls'. Says Naomi. 'Goodbye, auntie Yasmin. See you again soon!' Says Bella and Natasha – waving me goodbye and leaving. Then it's back to work for me, as I go and sing in front of thousands of people. Everyone's cheering and I love the feeling this gives me. I start off by singing my song, *"Just Want To be Loved",* and it goes like this: *"I just want you to cuddle me like a teddy bear. Just want you to stroke my hair. Show me that you care. Take me to the funfair. Don't just sit there, cuddle me like a teddy bear. Just want you to stroke my hair. I like you; I love you, I'm crazy about you. All I want and need is you. I know that you want me too, so let's just quit wasting time, and be with each other all of the time. I think about you all of the time. Time – so damn precious, and I want to spend every single second and minute of it with you. I don't want anyone else, I just want you, and I know that you want me too, so let's just quit wasting time, and be with each other all of the time. I think about you all of the time. You're on my mind all of the time. I want to be with you until the end of time. Cuddle me like a teddy bear, and stroke my hair. Take me to the funfair, because I just want to be loved by you, and spend the rest of my life with you. I'm crazy about you. All I want and need is you. I know that you want me too, so let's just quit wasting time, and be with each other all of the time. I think about you all of the time. You're on my mind all of the time. I want to be with you until the end of time. Cuddle me like a teddy bear, and stroke my hair, because I just want to be loved by you. I love you to the moon and back".*

Chapter ten: Dreaming, Believing and Receiving

Good news, it appears as though my visualising and believing stuff actually worked! I'm now in a relationship with a man who truly loves me and I honestly couldn't be happier! This man has been under my nose the whole entire time, and his name is Henry. Henry is the father of my child, and we decided to give things when the baby was born. We had a little boy named Christopher Peter Roberts. He's beautiful, happy and healthy. Henry is a great dad and even does the nappy (diaper) changes. Me and Henry are married now too, but that's not the only good news that I have to share... My sister, Naomi gave birth to beautiful twin boys. Bella and Natasha both wanted them to be girls so that they could dress them up in their doll's clothes. The twin boys, Billy and Nathan are a year old now, and my son Christopher Peter Roberts is twenty-one months old (so, nearly two years old now, basically). I'm pregnant with mine and Henry's second child. We're having a baby girl this time, so we'll have one of each. I'm still singing and song writing like I was before - performing in front of thousands of people. I've written two new songs. One is called *'Me'*, and it goes like this: *"Some people don't like me, but those people can bite me. I just wanna be around those who love me and accept me for who I am. Bang, bang, bang, slam. I don't give a damn, ma'am. Now why don't you just go off and drink your 'Baby Sham', like blam. You aren't part of my fam. You'll be waiting forever for me to give a damn about what you think of me. People shouldn't believe all of those things they hear about me, because those things you hear just ain't me. Don't blame me, blame the bitch that first started spreading shit about me in the fucking first place. Bitches like that don't even deserve a place at my dining room table, let alone in my life. Those types of people so need to get a motherfucking life and stay the fuck outta mine. I bet that some of those people can't even count to nine. They ain't ever coming round mine, because bitches like that don't even deserve a place at my dining room table, let alone in my life. Life is so very precious, so make sure you spend it around those who love you and accept you, and don't ever try to change you. Stay away from those who hate on you and disrespect you. Those type of people have no damn respect for anyone or anything – least of all you. Remember that you are better than them and better off without them. Life your life the way you want to, and now how other people want you to. It's your life and not theirs. Don't be like a flight of stairs and be walked all over. It's never too late to start over. Start from scratch if you must, but never ever give up. Keep your spirits up and keep a positive attitude and you'll be fine. Pretty soon, you'll have more than just a dime. Some things just take time. Remember that and take your time. Soon, it'll be your time to shine - shine like the morning sun. One day, you'll tell your future son all about this. Now, unclench your fist and write a list – a list of your goals and don't ever give up until you've achieved all of your goals. I believe in you, and so should you"* ... And the other is called: *"My Little Puppy"* and it goes like this: *"Puppy, I miss you. I miss looking at you, I miss cuddling you, I miss playing with you, I miss you so much. I want you back so much. I hate this so much, because sometimes, it all gets a little too much. I open your memory box, see your little collar and cry. I'd pay a million dollars if it meant that I could have you back – back at home with me just like the good old days. I feel so very lucky and so grateful to have had you until you were old. I got you when you were just a tiny, little puppy. You were so cute and so tiny. Your eyes were so bright and your fur was so shiny. You made everything feel alright and you didn't ever bite. The night before you died, I slept downstairs with you to spend one last precious night with you. You are missed so very much and that is true. You started off with those little blue eyes, but those blue eyes became brown eyes in the end. Oh, why did our time together ever have to come to an end? Puppy, I miss you. I miss looking at you, I miss cuddling you, I miss playing with you, I miss you so much. I want you back so much. Just to touch your silky, soft, shiny fur again would be so lovely. You are missed so very muchly, because you were, are and always will be my little puppy. Sleep tight. Oh, how I would love to hold you tight. You made everything feel alright and you didn't ever bite. I will never forget the night before you died, I slept downstairs with you to spend one last precious night with you. You looked at me and I looked at you. One day, I'll be back with you again and get to look, cuddle, play and spend time with you again, but until then, sleep tight, my sweet little puppy, and remember that I love you so very muchly" ...* I wrote this song about a dog I had a long time ago and how I felt after it passed away. He was called Harry. Me and my husband, Henry did think about adopting a dog, but with Christopher still being so young, and another child on the way, we thought that we'd wait a while before we do that. Plus, there's Naomi's little ones and I'm so busy with my singing career, that I worry that I won't be able to give it all of the love an attention that it deserves right now. I might just adopt one in the future, though. After all, the children won't stay children forever, will they? They grow up so fast. Once mine and Henry's baby daughter is born, our little family will be complete. We don't intend on having anymore children after her. We are done.

Lauren Abby has been writing stories since she was just a little girl. She has successfully written and published over one hundred books now, so be sure to check them all out! Just like this one, they are all available globally on Amazon in paperback and on Kindle.

Here's some other adult books also available by Lauren Abby that you'll also enjoy reading...

(All of these books are available globally on Amazon in paperback and on Kindle).

www.ingramcontent.com/pod-product-compliance
Lightning Source LLC
LaVergne TN
LVHW020544160826
845677LV00015B/4194

* 9 7 9 8 6 9 7 7 9 3 0 7 7 *